A Beginning,
a Muddle, and an End

A Beginning, a Muddle, and an End
The Right Way to Write Writing

AVI

WITH ILLUSTRATIONS BY
TRICIA TUSA

Harcourt, Inc.
Orlando   Austin   New York   San Diego   London

Requests for permission to make copies of any part of the work
should be submitted online at www.harcourt.com/contact or mailed
to the following address: Permissions Department, Harcourt, Inc.,
6277 Sea Harbor Drive, Orlando, Florida 32887-6777.

www.HarcourtBooks.com

Library of Congress Cataloging-in-Publication Data
Avi, 1937–
A beginning, a muddle, and an end: the right way
to write writing/Avi; illustrated by Tricia Tusa.
p. cm.
Summary: Avon the snail decides to become a writer with the help
of his friend Edward the ant, which leads them into a series of adventures
involving close encounters with an anteater, a tree frog, and a hungry fish.
[1. Authorship—Fiction.   2. Adventure and adventurers—Fiction.
3. Snails—Fiction.   4. Ants—Fiction.   5. Insects—Fiction.]
I. Tusa, Tricia, ill.   II. Title.
PZ7.A953Beg   2008
[E]—dc22   2007016580
ISBN 978-0-15-205555-4

Text set in Mrs. Eaves

First edition
A C E G H F D B

Printed in the United States of America

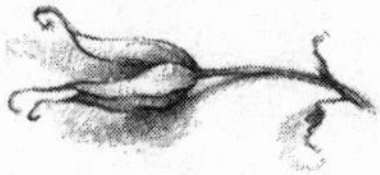

For Sarah, Sharon, Pam

Writers, A.R.T.ists, friends

Some time ago one of my young readers wrote to me about writing. Among the many wise things he said was that a good story consists of "a beginning, a muddle, and an end." It was the smartest description of a story I've ever read. I wish I knew his name. Perhaps he'll read this book. If so, I thank him for giving me a title.

—*Avi*

CHAPTER ONE

In Which Avon Feels Low

It was a dull, rainy morning, utterly gloomy.

Inside his house, Avon, a rather small snail, was staring at a blank piece of paper that stood before him. Across the room, his friend Edward the ant was lying on his back, staring up at the ceiling, which was just as blank.

Avon sighed. "The truth is, Edward," he said, "I've read a lot of adventures. And I've been on my own adventures. But I'm making no progress *writing* about my adventures."

"I'm so sorry to hear that," said Edward. "Do you know anything about why?"

"I'm pretty sure it's at the end of the alphabet," said Avon, "next to *Z*."

"I mean," said Edward, "that when writing goes poorly, it sometimes has to do with how you are feeling. Can you tell me how you *feel*?"

"Well, my spirits are . . . down."

"Avon, must I remind you? We live in a tree. You're actually up."

"Then how can I be so low?"

"Avon," said Edward, "would-be writers often think *attitude* is most important. More often than not, it's *altitude*."

"I've never looked at things that way," said Avon.

"Then it's time for you to look another way," suggested Edward. "After all, if you're looking down, it's only logical to assume you're up. But if you're looking up, you must be down. Still, I must advise you, some think it's best to be neither high nor low, but in the middle."

"I don't think," said Avon, "I've ever heard anyone say, 'I'm feeling *middle*.'"

"Perhaps you need to get a grip on yourself," said Edward.

"Edward!" cried Avon. "How can I get a grip when I have no hands?"

"My apologies," said Edward in haste. "I sometimes forget that we ants have a *lot* of hands."

"I always thought they were legs," said Avon.

"It depends."

"On what?"

"Sometimes it's better to have a leg up. Other moments it's good to be handy."

"My mother thought I was handsome," said Avon. "I've always tried to hold on to that. Will that get me anyplace?"

"Avon!" cried Edward. "Don't go *any*place. Go *some*place."

"What's wrong with *anyplace*?"

"You'll never find it on a map," said Edward.

"But what does *place* have to do with writing?"

"Avon," said Edward, "to write well, you need to know where you are going. My guess is that your writing has lost all sense of direction."

"It's hard for me to have a sense of direction," said Avon, "when I didn't even know I was supposed to go someplace."

"Avon, trust me. Great writing depends on your height: low, middle, or high."

"I'd like my writing to be right up there on the top," said Avon.

"Nothing could be easier," said Edward. "Because living where we do, as I've said, up in a tree, you're halfway there."

"Sounds like a plan," said Avon.

"Perfect," said Edward. "Because when it comes to writing, it's wise to start with a plan."

Avon brightened. "My plan has always been to write."

"Exactly," said Edward. "Write first. You can always figure out what you've written later."

CHAPTER TWO

In Which Avon Starts to Write

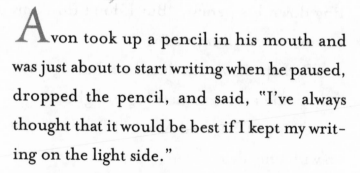

Avon took up a pencil in his mouth and was just about to start writing when he paused, dropped the pencil, and said, "I've always thought that it would be best if I kept my writing on the light side."

"Writing in the dark is harder," agreed Edward.

"Besides," said Avon, "if I wrote in the dark

and came upon something good, I'd probably miss it."

"I can see your point."

"Are you referring to my idea or my pencil?"

"Your bright idea."

"I like to think I'm bright," said Avon, putting down his pencil. "But I don't think my writing is very illuminating."

"Perhaps if we put our thoughts together, we'd come across something enlightening."

"Oh good!" agreed Avon. "I'll try to come up with one idea."

"And I," said Edward, "will try to come down with one."

"Then I hope," said Avon, "we'll meet in the middle."

After a few hours had passed, Avon asked, "Edward, did you think of anything yet?"

"Not a thing," said the ant.

"Perhaps," suggested Avon, "it would have been better if we had put *no* time into it. That way we could have come up with something timeless."

Edward said, "Avon you're so slow that in the time it takes you to say *now*, you might as well have said *then*. And by the time you notice the time is coming, it's generally past."

"I suppose," said Avon, "that's reaching a logical conclusion."

"Careful, Avon! If you've written a conclusion, you can't go any further."

"Not to worry. I don't want to write a conclusion, just a story."

"Let's agree then," said Edward, "that in regard to this story you're writing, if you're about to come to a conclusion, you'll head off in another direction. You might even find your own voice."

"It must be strange," mused Avon, "to be strolling about and suddenly come upon your voice just sitting there."

"I can only hope," said Edward, "it doesn't

speak a foreign language. By the way, Avon," added the ant, "this story you're going to write, is it a long or a short one?"

"I suppose that depends on how long it takes me to write it."

"Avon, the longer it takes to write a story, the shorter it takes to read."

"But I would never cut short my reading," said Avon.

"There's an old writer's saying: Never take shortcuts in your writing, but once you've written, it's wise to make lots of short cuts."

"But the short of it is, I'm still not sure how to begin," said Avon.

"You might start off on the right foot by writing *something*."

"Edward," said Avon, "considering I don't have feet, that would be quite a feat." But with much excitement, he picked up his pencil again and wrote: *Something*.

With much pride, he showed it to his friend. "What do you think?"

"Well, *Something* isn't *nothing*."

"Is it a start?"

"It could be an end."

"How can you tell the difference?" Avon asked.

"Look closely: Does it have anything to the left of it?"

"No."

"To the right?"

"No, again."

"In other words," said Edward, "it could be the beginning *or* the end of your book."

"Could it be that middle we were trying to reach?" Avon wanted to know.

"Let's hope not. Because if it is the middle, you'll have to put in words on *both* sides. On the other hand, if you wrote it as the beginning, you would only have to write the words on the right side."

"And if it's the end?" asked Avon.

"You'd need only to fill in the left side."

"Then let's forget about the middle," said Avon. "But which side will it be, the beginning or the end?"

"The writer always gets to decide."

"I think it would be more hopeful if *Something* was the beginning."

"Excellent! Then you only need to write on the right side."

"Edward!" cried Avon. "Think how many words you've saved me!"

CHAPTER THREE

*In Which Avon Gets a Lesson
in Punctuality*

Avon considered what he had written. *Something,* he decided, was a good beginning. But having begun, he did not know what to write next.

"Perhaps," he said, "my problem is that I don't know the correct *way* to write."

"There are many choices," said Edward. "You can go across the page, right to left, or left to right. Or, you could go up to down, or for that matter, down to up. Why, you could even write diagonally."

"But I wouldn't want to write down to anyone," said Avon.

"It would be depressing," agreed Edward.

"I want my writing to be elevating," said Avon.

"Living in this tree should give you lofty thoughts," Edward pointed out.

"True," said Avon, "and I like the idea of my writing being upbeat."

"So much better," agreed Edward, "than being beat-up."

"What about writing in circles?" asked Avon.

"Writers do that far too often," said Edward.

"But I'd like to be a well-rounded writer," said Avon.

"On the whole, yes," agreed Edward, "especially since it's not good to be considered square."

"And I'd like my book to be timely," said Avon.

"True," agreed Edward. "With as many deadlines as writers face, they need to be punctual."

"Then perhaps," said Avon, "I should begin my book with *Once upon a time*. Would that be punctual enough?"

"Avon," said Edward, "it's not being punctual that you need to worry about, but punctuation. Many writers think that when they write, it's the words that matter. Not at all. It's punctuation that's most important. All teachers of English should insist on that."

"They usually do," said Avon.

"They should," said Edward. "Listen to this." He put one of his legs over his heart and proclaimed: "Avon! Don't forget all I said. You must not! Speak the truth about what happened! Things will be better, I think. To lie about the truth, it *never* helps!"

"I agree with every word," said Avon.

"Every *word*?" asked Edward. "Because you might want to put it this way: "Avon, don't! Forget all I said. You must not speak the truth about what happened. Things *will* be! Better, I think, to lie. About the truth . . . It never helps!"

Avon was astonished. "They seem like the same words!" he cried.

"They are."

"But they mean the opposite."

"Avon! Be careful. A good writer will never say mean things. But the best mean what they say."

"But if you've reached the mean," said Avon, "you're back in the middle."

"Which is the reason," Edward pointed out, "why punctuation is the secret to great writing. A writer who isn't punctual is never quite in step with the time."

Avon became alarmed. "But, Edward, you know snails can never be in step. We have no feet or, for that matter, shoes. We just sort of *slip* along."

"Sounds like slipshod writing."

"That's not a very neat idea," Avon said. "I'll have to do better."

"Exactly," agreed Edward. "In writing, telling what you're going to write is never as exciting as the *doing*."

"Why?"

"It's the way good writers pay their dues."

CHAPTER
FOUR

In Which Avon Chooses a Profession

Avon spent much of that day gazing at the sheet of paper before him, staring at the one word he'd written: *Something*.

"Edward," he finally said, "do you remember when you told me about the need for writers to be punctual?"

"That was a short time ago."

"All the same, I've been thinking about it.

Since writing is so hard, perhaps instead of be-coming a writer, I should become an author."

"Avon, you can't become an author until you first become a writer."

"Why is that?"

"A writer is someone who tries to get the words right. That's why they are called writers. But an *author* is someone who has written the words wrong. Any critic will tell you that."

"Is it hard to write right?"

"If a writer isn't right, he's bound to be left behind."

"I'd still like to try."

"What will you write?"

"That's my biggest worry. I'm afraid I've not had an exciting life."

"Then write about what you haven't done."

"Is that allowed?" asked Avon.

"You should know that the number one rule about writing is: Write what you know. So if you know what you haven't done, write about that."

"What if you don't know what you've not done?"

"Then you go on to rule number two."

"Which is?"

"Write about what you don't know."

"Is there a third rule?"

"Yes, stories do usually have three rules. Rule number three is: Write about what you don't know as if you *did* know about it."

"Any fourth rule?"

"Absolutely: Make sure that when you're writing about what you don't know as if you did know, conceal the fact that you don't know what you're doing."

"Is there a fifth rule?"

"A crucial one. It's: Always leave your readers guessing."

"Guessing what?"

"Let them guess about which parts you know, which parts you don't know, and which parts you don't know but are writing as if you did know."

"What if they guess right?"

"I told you, the one who is righter becomes a writer."

"What if they're wrong?"

"That's the moment you become an author."

"Sounds like it takes a lot of work to be a writer."

"You're never wronger than when you decide to become a writer."

"Edward, I hope you're not offended, but I'm not so sure *wronger* is a word."

"You're probably right."

"Or wrong."

"Whatever works," agreed Edward.

"Edward," said Avon with a sigh, "maybe I shouldn't be a writer *or* an author. I had no idea it would be so hard."

"Be a reader then."

"Is that easier?"

"Actually, it's much harder."

"I don't understand," said Avon.

"Avon, what's writing? Scribbled letters on paper. It's the reader who has to make sense of it."

"I know writers used to be paid by how many words they wrote," said Avon, "so I suppose the more they wrote, the more cents they made. Which to me makes very little sense."

"Actually," explained Edward, "it depends on what kind of writer you are. What kind were you intending to be?"

"A writer who attracts readers."

"Then for heaven's sake, don't write writing. Write reading."

CHAPTER FIVE

In Which Avon and Edward Do Nothing

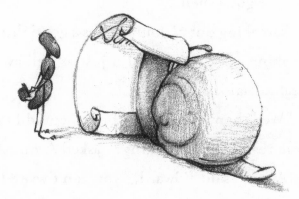

By the next day Avon had still written only one word: *Something.* After much thought about what else he might write, he announced, "Edward, I think I need a break."

"All very nice for you to say," objected Edward. "As you've constantly reminded me, you don't have arms or legs. Nothing much for you to break."

"I've got a shell."

"Breaking out of your shell is a good thing. Breaking a leg is *not.* So I'll just as well avoid breaks, thank you."

"Well then, instead of a break, could I take some rest from my writing?" asked Avon.

"Avon," said Edward, "you can't write the rest unless you have written *some.*"

"Some what?"

"Whatever you wanted to write more of."

"But I've written only one word," said Avon.

"Look at it this way," said Edward. "If what you're writing will have only two words, then you've written half."

"What could I write that has only two words?"

"A very, very short story."

"Could you give me an example?" asked Avon.

Edward thought for a moment. "Here's one: 'He died.'"

"That doesn't seem very lively," said Avon.

"Then you've understood the story perfectly," said Edward.

Avon sighed. "I think resting would suit me best."

"Do that and you'll be the first snail I've ever seen wearing a suit," said Edward.

Avon put his pencil aside, lowered his head, and closed his eyes. But after a while he sighed. "I have to admit, Edward, doing nothing makes me restless."

"That's because you can't *do* nothing."

"I can't?" said a startled Avon.

"You can *do* your writing. You can *do* a dance. You can even *do* smart things. But I don't see how you can *do* nothing. Because if you're *doing* nothing," explained Edward, "then you must be *doing* something, which is certainly *not* doing . . . well . . . *nothing*."

"Edward!" cried Avon. "I've been doing nothing for most of my life!"

"No wonder you're exhausted," said Edward.

"Do you have a suggestion?"

"Try doing *something*," suggested Edward. "I think you'll find it much more enjoyable."

"I did write *Something*," said Avon.

"Well then, *do* something with it."

"What exactly could I do?"

"Try thinking about nothing."

"Isn't that hard?"

"Nothing to be taken lightly."

"What about heavy thoughts?"

"Only if you have strong feelings."

"I'll try," said Avon, and almost immediately cleared his throat, his ears, his eyes, and his mind of everything.

Edward waited patiently. After a couple of hours went by, he asked, "Avon?"

"Yes, Edward."

"Are you thinking about anything?"

"I'm thinking about not thinking. But it worries me."

"Why?"

"Because my father always told me not to be thoughtless."

"And *my* father always taught me that it's the thought that counts."

"I'd much prefer that."

"Why?"

"Because I've always been good at mathematics. So if it's one's thoughts that count, my writing might add up to more than *Something*."

"That," agreed Edward, "figures."

CHAPTER
SIX

In Which Edward Offers a Song

The next day, when Avon woke up, he said, "Oh, Edward, I feel so dismal about my writing."

"Have you actually been writing, then?"

"No, just talking about it."

"Not to worry," said Edward. "Most writers talk about writing way more than they actually write. Then, when they finally *do* write, they mostly write talk, not writing. So maybe I can cheer you up. Do you remember how I once taught you some songs?"

"Faintly," said Avon.

"Loud songs, actually," said Edward. "And I know they were good songs, but in the end they were ant songs. The point is, I've been writing a snail song. It's meant to cheer you up."

"Edward," cried Avon, "how thoughtful of you to up the ante! I'd love to hear it."

"It's not quite finished," said Edward. "But so far here's the way it goes." The ant took a deep breath and began to sing:

> *"This is a snail song because*
> *It takes sooooooooooooooooooooooo-*
> *oooooooooooooooo long to sing.*

That's because snail songs

Take a looooooooooooooooooooooooooooo–

oooooooooooooong, long time to sing.

Because if a snail song didn't take

Soooooooooooooooooooooooooooooooooooooooo

Long to sing, it wouldn't really be a snail

Soooooooooooooooooooooooooooo–

ooooooooooooooooong!"

Edward looked at his friend. "What do you think?"

"I think snails might like it a lot," said Avon. "It has a very catchy melody."

"Do you think it needs work?" asked Edward.

"I can make one suggestion . . ."

"Please."

"There may be too many *o*'s."

"You might be right," said Edward. "Maybe if you sang it, I could get a better sense of that."

"Happy to give it a try," said Avon. He began to sing:

"This is a snail song because
It takes sooooooooooooooooooooooooo-
oooooooooooooooo long to sing.
That's—"

"Hold it!" cried Edward.

"What's the matter?" asked Avon.

"When you got to the 'soooooooooooooooooo-oooooooooooooooooooooooo' part, you left out one of the *o*'s."

"I did?"

"I'm afraid so."

"I'm very sorry," said Avon. "Let me try it again." Taking a deep breath, he started to sing the song a second time:

> *This is a snail song because*
> *It takes soooooooooooooooooooooooo-*
> *ooooooooooooooooo long to sing.*
> *That's—*

"Forgive me, Avon." Edward felt obliged to cut in. "That time you *added* an *o*."

"Edward, are you absolutely sure?"

"No question about it. I mean, I wrote that song, so I can tell when others get it wrong."

"Well, no offense," said Avon, "but—does it really matter?"

"Of course it does."

"Why?"

"Because if you sing it differently than I do, it's really two songs."

"Would that be so wrong?" asked Avon.

"Two songs don't make it right," said Edward.

"And that," agreed Avon, "most certainly would be wrong."

CHAPTER SEVEN

In Which Avon and Edward Have a Few Words

The next day Avon was resting after many hours of thinking about what else he might write on the piece of paper that lay before him other than the *Something* he'd already written.

"Edward," he announced, "I think I'm hungry."

"Would that," asked Edward, "be hungry for ideas, new words, or—?"

"Stomach hungry, actually. Only I don't see much to eat."

"Yes, I'm afraid our kitchen is empty," said Edward. "So you might have to eat your words."

"I'd be happy to, except I've only written one word," said Avon. "I was hoping for more nourishment. Could you recommend a particularly good word?"

Edward thought for a while. Then he said, "I've always liked *raddle.*"

"What's it mean?"

"It's an old-fashioned word for *red.*"

Avon shook his head. "Too rare for me," he said.

"Then how do you like your meat?"

"Actually, I find meetings boring," replied Avon. "I'd rather make myself a leaf sandwich."

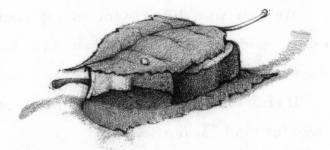

"How do you do that?"

"It's a piece of bread between two leaves."

"Might I suggest you turn over a new leaf?" said Edward.

"Edward," said Avon, "I simply want a bite to eat."

"These days creatures seem to be content

with sound bites," said Edward. "Yet sound bites are rarely sound."

"That still leaves me hungry."

"Well, if you didn't want to eat your words," said Edward, "there's always food for thought."

"If I had some thoughts, I'd gladly exchange them for food," said Avon.

"Then you'd become thought-full."

"Edward," said Avon, "you are my best friend, but sometimes I think you try too hard to be clever."

Edward became raddled with embarrassment. "Avon," he said, "a word to the wise is sufficient."

Avon thought for a while, and then he said,

"Edward, what wise word would that actually be?"

Edward shrugged all of his shoulders. "Creatures have spent years trying to discover that word. I'm not so sure there is one."

"Edward," said Avon, "those are the wisest words you've ever said."

CHAPTER EIGHT

*In Which Avon and Edward
Have a Spell of Spelling*

After having spent yet another day writing nothing, Avon decided he needed some fresh air. Edward was agreeable. So the two friends stepped out of their house, only to have Avon suddenly say, "Edward, look over there! Unless I miss my guess—"

"Avon," said Edward, "if you practiced your guessing, you wouldn't miss so much."

"What I was trying to say, Edward, before you interrupted me, is that I think an anteater is coming our way."

"An anteater! Why is he on a tree?"

"Since you're an ant, I suppose it's because of you."

"Then I have no intention of staying here."

"Edward," said Avon, "don't be frightened. I think I can protect you."

"How are you going to do that?"

"I suppose being a writer has something to do with spelling. So I intend to save you from this anteater with spelling."

"I had no idea you were a good speller."

"I know all my letters by heart," said Avon.

"Avon, in all the time I've known you, I've

never seen you receive so much as one letter. So your alphabet can't be very complete."

"Not only is it complete, I can arrange the letters, too. For example, I know the difference between g-o-d and d-o-g."

"You have things backward," said Edward.

"Edward!" cried Avon. "I'm trying to be straightforward."

"You think you're smart," said Edward, "but in ancient Egypt they worshipped a god named Anubis who *was* a dog. So if you lived then, the difference between spelling g-o-d and d-o-g wouldn't have been helpful. You could have spelled the word in either direction and you'd get the same thing, a dog *and* a god."

"That sounds like religious dogma," said Avon. "Edward, you simply are going to have to trust me."

In fact, the anteater was approaching rapidly, his long, sticky tongue constantly poking about.

"Edward!" cried Avon. "Hurry! Get behind me!"

"Avon," said a frightened Edward, "I just hope you know how to spell."

"Don't worry," returned Avon. "I intend to do what I'm hoping."

"But what you're doing and what I'm hoping, and what I'm doing and what you're hoping, may be four different things," said Edward from behind.

"Shhh!" said Avon. "He's here."

The anteater lumbered up to Avon and stopped. "I beg your pardon," he said. "I'm quite sure an ant was here a moment ago. Perhaps you can tell me where he went."

"What did you want him for?" asked Avon.

"What do you think? I am an anteater. I'm hungry. And I eat ants."

"Excuse me for asking," said Avon, "but how do you spell that?"

"Spell what?"

"What you eat."

"Ant. A-n-t."

"I don't wish to alarm you," said Avon, "but I think you're making a huge mistake. I think it's an aunt—a-u-n-t—that you like to eat."

The anteater was startled. "Are you suggesting I've been eating the wrong thing all my life?" he cried.

"I'm afraid so."

"I'm feeling sick," said the anteater, sucking his tongue back into his mouth with a slurp.

"Maybe you'd best go to a doctor and get an antidote."

The anteater started to turn around, only to stop. "Wait a minute," he said, looking back. "Can't an ant be an aunt?"

"I suppose," admitted Avon.

"What about that ant I just saw here—an aunt or an uncle?"

"I assure you," said Avon, "that ant will never become an aunt."

"I do beg your pardon," said the anteater, and he waddled away in search of an aunt to eat.

A very happy Edward came out from behind Avon's shell. "Avon," he cried, "you're a genius! It was as if you put a spell upon that creature."

"It just goes to show," agreed Avon, "that in this world *U* can make a difference."

CHAPTER NINE

In Which Avon and Edward
Get into an Argument

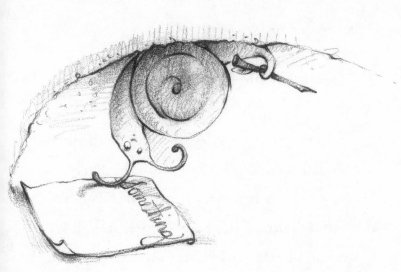

Having dealt with the aunt eater, Avon went back inside to write. He stared at the paper—which still had only *Something* on it—and by the next morning he suddenly had an idea. "Edward?" he called.

"Yes, Avon?"

"How long have we known each other?"

"Are you counting minutes, days, or years?" asked Edward.

"Don't they add up to the same thing?" said Avon.

"There are always fewer years than min-utes," Edward said. "But though there are fewer, a year is too long to think about. On the other hand, I find days much too short. I much prefer thinking about months. There's something comforting about the word *month*."

"*Month* always reminds me of *munch*," said Avon. "And *munch* reminds me of *lunch*. And that reminds me that one of these days we should eat."

"But to get back to your question," said Edward. "I have a hunch we've known each other for a bunch of months. What makes you ask?"

"In all that time," said Avon, "we've never had an argument."

"It's a curious thing about arguments," said Edward. "While creatures often lose arguments, I've never heard of anyone *getting* an argument."

"And more curiously," agreed Avon, "even if you don't have one, you can still get *into* one."

"It would have to be large enough to contain two creatures," said Edward, "since you can't very well get into an argument all by yourself. Why are you so interested in arguments?"

"My idea," said Avon, "is that if we had an argument, I could write about it. Do you know what an argument might cost?"

"It might cost us our friendship."

"I don't want that!" cried Avon.

"Actually," said Edward, "arguments come cheap: Which is to say, they don't take much to keep alive. Give an argument a little bit to chew on every once in a while, and it will live for a long time. My parents had an argument that went on for years."

"What was it about?"

"He said she liked to argue. She said she didn't. It was something they often disagreed about. The point being, while some arguments grow old, they rarely change. In fact, the longer they hang around, the less likely *anything* will change."

"My point is," Avon reminded his friend,

"we don't have one. Perhaps that's why I can't write. Every story needs some tension, but there's no tension in my life. It makes me very tense."

"If we had an argument," asked Edward, "what would you like it to be about?"

"Do we have a choice?"

"It probably wouldn't be helpful to argue about things upon which we agree," said Edward.

"No argument there," said Avon.

"My point exactly. So, just go ahead and say something," suggested Edward. "I'll disagree, and then, there you are, we'll have our very own argument. Then you can write about it."

"What if you agree with what I say?"

"Just pick something that's easy to argue about."

Avon became thoughtful. "Got it!" he cried out after a while. "Let's have an argument about breathing."

"Breathing?"

"I think it's a good thing," said Avon. "What do you think?"

"Many things," said Edward.

"Edward," said Avon, "you're supposed to disagree."

"I can't argue about *breathing*!"

"You could if you wanted to."

"Avon, nobody would say breathing is *bad* for you."

"A rock might."

"Why would a rock say that?"

"Because rocks don't breathe. I've always assumed it's because they don't like it."

"Avon," cried Edward, "rocks don't think, or talk. Why are you grinning?"

"I think we've found an argument."

"Good. Then go write about it. The truth is, arguments make me sleepy."

"I won't disagree," said Avon. He thought for a bit, and then he wrote.

"Edward, I think I've got a title for my

book. I'm going to call it *The Little Rock That Didn't Like to Breathe.*"

"What would happen in the story?"

"The rock would hold its breath."

"For how long?"

"Until it changed its mind."

"Forgive me, Avon, but rocks don't have minds. They are thoughtless."

"Really?"

"No question about it."

"That explains it."

"Explains what?"

"For years I've talked to rocks. When they didn't answer, I always thought they just didn't want to speak to me. Now you say they are thoughtless. I certainly don't want to write about rude rocks!"

And he scratched out his title.

CHAPTER
TEN

In Which Edward and Avon
Remember Something They Forgot

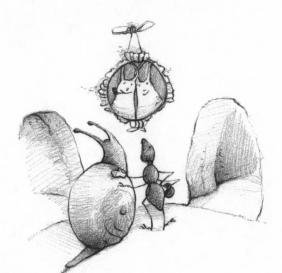

"Wait a minute!" cried Edward. "We've talked a whole lot about writing, but we've said nothing about your grammar."

"She was a very nice creature."

"What about your grandpa?"

"He was nice, too."

Edward nodded. "I suppose one's grammar is always relative."

CHAPTER
ELEVEN

*In Which Avon and Edward
Observe a Nest*

Two days later, in the early evening, Edward was on the back porch, resting from a day of doing nothing.

Avon came out of their house. "Another frustrating day!" exclaimed the snail. "I still can't find anything to write about."

"Avon," Edward whispered, "look over there," and he pointed with four of his legs.

"That bundle of twigs and leaves," said Edward.

"How come we never noticed it before?" wondered Avon.

"We've been looking for ideas, not twigs and leaves. Creatures usually only see what they are looking for."

"Are you suggesting we should look for what we don't see?"

"You can see more that way," suggested Edward.

"But that thing just looks like a confused mess," said Avon.

"Actually," said Edward, "I think it's a nest."

Sure enough, as they looked on, a crow popped her head up and stared at them with beady black eyes.

"We beg your pardon," said Avon. "We didn't know anyone was here."

"Where else do you think I'd be?" asked the crow. "If I'm not there, it's more than likely that I'll be here."

"You could be someplace else," suggested Edward.

"But that snail already said I was here," said

the crow. "And since I'm not anyplace else, here I am. In fact, this is my nest, and I've been sitting on my egg for fourteen days."

"Isn't that hard?" asked the snail.

"Eggs are always hard," said the crow. "But if you want children, you have to sit on them. That's why parents have such a hard life."

"I'm not sure I understand," said Avon.

"An egg is not likely to grow on its own," said the crow crossly.

"She's right," said Edward. "I've never seen a grown-up egg."

"The egg doesn't grow!" cried the bird. "It's what's inside that grows."

"Then why don't you sit on what's inside?" Avon asked.

"Because there's a shell."

"What makes you so sure there's something inside?" asked Edward.

"It's always been that way!" insisted the crow.

"Do you know what's inside?"

"I am hatching a baby crow," said the bird indignantly.

"Perhaps it's a story," said Avon with great interest. "I've heard of creatures hatching plots. I could use one."

"That would be poaching," said Edward.

"I hate poached eggs," said the crow.

"Forgive me for asking," asked Edward, "but if you're sitting on the egg, how will you know when it's ready?"

"I'll know," said the crow, "when the egg cracks."

"Being a parent," Edward scolded, "is not a laughing matter. These days an egg in the nest *requires* a nest egg."

"But that's so very costly!" protested the crow.

"My point," cried Edward, "eggs-actly!"

The crow sighed. "I'm just going to have to wing it."

"You know," said Avon as the two friends returned to their house, "for that bird's sake I can only hope being a parent is what it's cracked up to be."

CHAPTER
TWELVE

In Which Avon and Edward
Learn a Rule

It was early in the morning two days later, and Avon was out on the porch taking a break from not writing. Edward was there to help.

Suddenly Edward cried, "Avon, look out!"

A startled Avon looked around. Not far from the two friends, a large, spotted green tree frog was glaring at them.

"What are you doing here?" asked the tree frog.

"I'm trying to write a story," said Avon.

"How long?" demanded the frog.

"Story or writing or trying?" asked Avon.

"What difference does that make?" said the frog. "The point is, did you get my permission to do it?"

"I don't think he needs anyone's approval to write a story," put in Edward.

"That's a likely story!" cried the frog. "Because he *does* need permission since among the three of us, I'm the biggest. Therefore, I'm in charge."

"There's nothing reasonable about that at all," retorted Edward. "The only thing you're bigger than, here, is us."

"Us is enough for me," insisted the tree frog. "Bigger means best."

"Does that mean best means bigger?" asked Avon.

"Bigger—better, it's the same thing," said the tree frog.

"They *are* different words," Avon pointed out.

"Nonsense!" cried the tree frog. "Since they have the same number of letters, they are equal."

"*Lots* and *none* have equal letters," Edward protested. "But they are unequal."

"And," said Avon, "*huge* and *large* have different numbers of letters, but they pretty much mean the same thing."

"Both words end in an *e*," said the tree frog. "Which is why they almost have the same meaning."

"Hold on!" cried Avon. "Politely and rudely both end in a *y*. Are you saying they're the same?"

"You're just playing with words," said the tree frog, puffing herself up. "I repeat, the important question is, who is bigger?"

"Sometimes," Edward pointed out, "small is bigger if you compare small things with even smaller things."

"Don't try to confuse me with logic," said the tree frog. "The only things I hate more than logic are facts that tell me I'm wrong."

"What about facts that tell you you're right?"

"This being a free country," said the tree frog, "I don't care what you say as long as I get to decide which facts are right and which are wrong."

"That doesn't seem fair," said Avon.

"Not a fact!" objected the tree frog.

"I think we're right," said Edward.

"The fact is," said the tree frog, "a fact isn't a fact unless someone—meaning me—decides it is a fact."

"And where do you get *your* facts?" asked Edward.

"I make them at a factory."

Avon said, "Well, my fact is, I am going to write a story, and I don't think I need your permission to do so."

"Not so fast!" cried the tree frog.

"Oh, you needn't worry about that," said Avon. "I am writing very slowly."

"You are talking to me," said the tree frog. "That's the only fact I approve of."

"Well then," said Edward, "prove it."

"Your friend here"—the tree frog nodded to Avon—"claimed two things. First he said he was writing a story. Well, look at him. Is he writing? No. He's talking. He's just a talker who *thinks* he's a writer. Then he said he didn't need my permission to write or talk. That's not a fact, either."

"Is that your proof?" said Edward.

"Must I say it again: The only proof I need is that I'm the biggest creature around here."

"And I say again," exclaimed Avon, "that's size, not fact!"

"Right," said Edward. "In any case, you're not bigger than the tree."

"And the tree isn't bigger than the forest," added Avon.

"And the forest isn't bigger than the world," said Edward.

"And the last time I looked," Avon pointed out, "the world isn't bigger than the universe, though I'm willing to admit I've never actually measured it."

"Right," said Edward. "So if the biggest thing gets to decide what a fact is, I have to ask if it's a fact that you got permission from the universe to ask permission of us?"

"Well . . . no," admitted the tree frog.

"Don't you think you should factor that in?" said Avon.

"I . . . don't know how to talk to the

universe," said the rather embarrassed frog.

"Excuse me," said Edward. "But if you look right behind you, there's a robin. The way she's gazing at you with her open beak—this is just my opinion, not yet a fact—I think she's considering eating you."

The tree frog glanced over her shoulder, saw the robin, and immediately leaped away to safety.

Avon and Edward watched her go.

Then Edward said, "Do you know, Avon, what I've noticed is that there's always something bigger than something."

"Unless it's smaller than something," said Avon.

"That's called a measured response," agreed

Edward. "Which means that the only rule for things is—there's no need to have a ruler."

"Good gracious!" cried Avon. "Then everything is always bigger and smaller at the same time!"

"Exactly. Wherever you go, you're always in the middle."

"Edward!" cried Avon. "Now I understand why I haven't been able to write. I always thought the way to start off was to write the beginning. I now realize I can put an end to my writing problems by starting to write in the middle!"

Very excited, Avon took up his pencil and wrote the word—*Something*—right in the middle of a fresh piece of paper.

"Avon!" exclaimed Edward. "Once again you've written *Something* very well!"

CHAPTER THIRTEEN

*In Which Avon and Edward
Are Blown Away*

Avon stared at what he had written for a long time. "I have to admit," he said, "what I've done is not very good. In the end, though I have composed the middle, it's only a beginning."

"I suggest you consider it a first draft," said Edward.

Avon looked around. The leaves and

branches of their tree were certainly being tossed about. "It *is* a drafty evening," he said.

"Very few writers get away with just writing *Something*," said Edward.

"The truth is," admitted Avon, "I've not gotten away at all. In fact, I've gotten nowhere."

"Writers usually need to do some rewriting," said Edward.

"Do you really think so?"

"It's the way professional writers work," said Edward.

With a sigh, Avon picked up his pencil and wrote *Something* in the middle of the paper five more times. He showed the paper to Edward. "Have I rewritten it enough times?"

"Avon, just because you've rewritten *Something* doesn't mean it's *anything*," said Edward.

"Edward, if I wanted to write *anything*, I wouldn't have written *Something*."

Edward held up a leg and measured the wind. "More drafts," he said.

"I'm afraid," Avon said, "I don't have a way with words."

"Avon, by now you should know that words don't really weigh anything. In fact, the way this wind is coming on, your words are likely to get blown away."

"At least my writing would get someplace," said Avon. "Which is more than I can say for myself. The truth is, Edward, all this failure is making me feel quite edgy."

Edward became alarmed. "Just how many edges do you have?"

"Does it matter?"

"Get twelve edges and you're a block. Being blocked is very common to writers. Perhaps that's your problem."

A tear gathered in one of Avon's eyes. "I suppose I've gone as far as I can go."

"But going as far as you can go," said Edward, "means that as far as you are concerned, you've gone nowhere."

"But look!" said Avon. "There's sky above us. And clouds. Lots of wind. And what about the sun? What's the point of my being at my top if there is so much more on top of me?"

"Try looking at things sideways."

Avon did so, staring out over the forest. "Edward, now all I can see is more leaves and bark."

"Avon, do I have to remind you: You're not barking up the wrong tree, you're writing. Just remember the old saying about not seeing the forest for the trees."

Avon thought for a while, and then, as he continued to look about, he said, "It seems to me that even if I were to be in a different tree, I'd have the same sky, clouds, and sun over me."

"That's because even when you get to the top, you're always below something."

Avon looked down. "I have to admit, it does look as if there's more down there than up here. Does that mean the higher you go, the less there is?"

"Avon, that's what I'd call downright smart!"

"Do you really think so?"

"Avon, it appears that you've gotten to the bottom of things at last! I suggest you try one more draft."

Avon bit down on his paper and held it up.

But right then a strong puff of wind caught it like a sail and blew him—and his writing—off the tree.

Not pausing for an instant, the ever-loyal Edward dived right off after him.

CHAPTER
FOURTEEN

*In Which Avon and Edward Fall
into an Argument*

Avon and Edward were falling.

"What are you doing here?" asked Avon from midair.

"I always think it's good for old friends to catch up," said Edward.

"Edward!" cried Avon as he tumbled. "I can't see you very well."

"Don't worry. I can see you."

"Where are you?"

"Not very far from where you are."

"What do I look like?"

"Pretty much the same as always," said Edward. "Only now you're up in the air."

Avon did a flip. "Ah, there you are. But, oh gosh, Edward, you're upside down."

"Actually," returned Edward, "I think it's you that's been turned around."

"Edward, I'm sure it's you," said Avon.

"But," said Edward, "I'm just as convinced it's you."

"Edward!" cried Avon with excitement. "We're finally having a falling-out!"

"We can't argue about which way is up or down," returned Edward.

"Are you telling me you're not up for it?" asked Avon.

"No! I'm saying if you're upside down," said Edward, "then down is up and up is down. It's all about how you're standing."

"But, Edward," said Avon, "I assure you, at the moment I don't stand for anything. In fact, I'm falling."

"Actually, you seem to be falling all over yourself."

"Which way? Up or down?" asked Avon.

"Avon," said Edward, "you can't really believe that up is down and down is up, can you? Until now up was *always* up and down was *always* down."

"Not if you're upside down," insisted Avon.

"Avon, you have a twisted way of thinking."

"Your way is backward!"

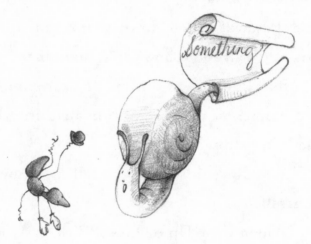

Even as he spoke, the wind turned him over again. "Ah," said Avon. "Edward, I must apologize. You're right. Up is down and down is up."

But Edward, who also had rolled over, said, "That's very upright of you, Avon, but it's you who are correct. I can see it now. Down is up and up is down."

"I don't think this is getting us anywhere," said Avon.

"Yes, it is," said Edward.

"Where?" said Avon.

"We're falling," said Edward.

"Which direction?" asked Avon.

Edward looked about. "It's either up or down," he suggested.

"Well," said Avon, "since we are so confused, it's a good thing we can have only two choices.

"But on the whole," he added as he, his

friend, and his writing continued to tumble down through the air, "I'd rather rise to the occasion."

"Being such good friends," agreed Edward, "I certainly don't wish to fall apart."

Sure enough they continued to drift down.

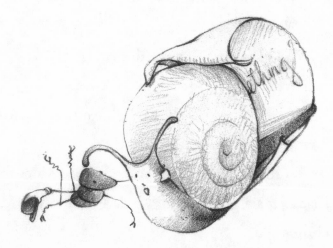

"Edward," cried Avon, "what's going to happen to us? There's nothing for us to do!"

"I wouldn't say *nothing*," said Edward, pointing to Avon's writing, which was fluttering down not far from where they were. "That's what's so wonderful about writing. We've always got *Something* to read."

CHAPTER FIFTEEN

In Which the Question, to Sea or Not to See, Is Reviewed

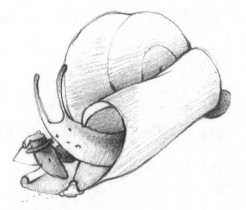

As the wind continued to toss Edward and Avon, as well as the paper Avon had been writing on, Avon managed to stretch his neck out, take hold of the paper with his mouth, and pull himself onto it. Edward, who was close, pulled himself onto it, too.

"It's good to have *Something* solid beneath us," said Avon as they drifted through the air.

"I'm not so sure," said Edward, who was peering cautiously over the edge. "Things might not go so well if what we land on is harder than what we're flying on."

"I didn't find *Something* that hard to write," Avon said. "What do you see down there?"

"The world."

"That seems like a good place to go."

"But at the moment," said Edward, "all I'm seeing below is sea."

"Did you say you're seeing sea?"

"It's hardly a secret. Look! There are two seagulls flying by."

"Is the second one a sequel?" asked Avon. "Sequels make me seasick."

"If you get sick of seeing," said Edward, "try looking at things with your eyes closed."

"It's hard to keep an open mind with your eyes closed," said Avon. "What will we do when we land?"

"If it is land, I won't have a sinking feeling," said Edward.

"But what if we bounce?" asked Avon.

"Life is full of ups and downs!"

"I'm hoping for the first!" cried Avon.

Nevertheless, they continued descending. It took so long that Avon said, "Edward, I'm *really* hungry."

Edward stole another look at the sea. "I don't know about food, but in a few moments there will be a lot of seasoning."

"Actually, my favorite season is summer."

"Too bad, because right now it's nothing but fall."

"Being dropped this way," sighed Avon, "makes me want to have a more grounded life."

"Too late for that," said Edward. Sure enough, within moments the paper fluttered gently down and landed on the sea. There it floated, bobbing aimlessly on the waves.

Edward considered what Avon had written. "Here's hoping we have *Something* going for us."

"I'm so sorry, Edward," said Avon. "This is all my fault. If I had never written *Something,* this wouldn't have happened. I hope we don't sink. Being at the bottom would top everything."

"If we do go under," said Edward as he gazed into the ocean, "I only hope we can rise to the occasion."

Even as he spoke, an enormous fish poked his head out of the water and stared at them. "Who are you?" he demanded.

"Avon Snail, at your service," said Avon.

"Edward Ant," said Edward. "But I am not at your service."

"Are you eatable?" asked the fish.

"Actually," said Avon, "I was only just saying I haven't eaten in a long time."

"Neither have I," said Edward.

"Well," said the fish as he opened his mouth very wide, "now you can say you've been eaten," and he swallowed the two friends in one great gulp.

CHAPTER SIXTEEN

In Which Avon and Edward Are Kept in the Dark

It was very dark inside the fish. Avon looked this way and that, but could not find Edward. Then he heard, "Avon?"

"Is that you, Edward?"

"I think so," said Edward. "But Avon, is that you?"

"As far as I can see."

"Just how far *can* you see?" asked Edward.

"I've been told I'm far-fetched, but that's not very far at all."

"That's exactly what I'm seeing."

"At least we're seeing eye to eye."

"But I can't see your eyes. I can't even see my own eyes."

"I've never been able to see my eyes," said Avon. "Are they worth looking at?"

"If not *at,* certainly *with.*"

"Where do you think we are?" Avon asked.

"I'm afraid I'm in the dark," said Edward. "But I don't mind being in the dark as much as I mind being kept in the dark."

"Do you think the whole world has turned dark?"

"Maybe since we're inside a fish, it's just dark here."

"You mean, outside the fish . . . ?"

"I suppose there's light. Unless the water's dark."

"It could be nighttime," said Avon.

"Wise creatures," said Edward, "always say you should look inside yourself to find the light."

"Is that what's meant by *insight*?"

"Perhaps light-headed. But in the end, being light-footed might be of more help," said Edward.

"Must I remind you one more time," said Avon a little peevishly, "I don't have feet."

"You may have no feet," said Edward, "but I have six. If we average them out, we'll each have three."

"Who said that?" boomed a voice.

"It's so dark I can't tell who's talking."

"It's not the kind of thing *I* would say."

"I wouldn't say it, either."

"Maybe somebody else said it."

"What happens if it wasn't one of us?"

"You might consider writing about it."

"I'd like to write about what I've seen, but I haven't seen anything."

"Use your imagination to come up with something."

"When the fish swallowed us, I left *Something* behind."

"Would you please stop talking!" came the booming voice again.

"Was that you?"

"No, was it you?"

"That depends on who *you* is. If it's you it can't be me."

"But if it is me, it can't be you."

"I think we'd better ask who it is."

"Hello there! Would you please say whether it's you or me who's talking?"

"It's me! The fish."

"Are you me or you?"

"Me!"

"Are you the one who swallowed us?"

"Who else could it be?"

"Since I can't see anything, I suppose it

could be any number of creatures. Have you swallowed anyone else lately?"

"Just you."

"What about me?"

"I like to eat intelligently, but if I'd known what the two of you were going to say, I wouldn't have swallowed you. Neither of you seems very bright."

"Then let me enlighten you," said Edward. "We're in the dark."

"But you could always spit us out!" called Avon.

"I'll be happy to. I could use some inner peace."

"I guess," Avon whispered to Edward, "he doesn't realize what small pieces we are."

The next moment Avon and Edward were spit out of the fish's mouth and onto what felt like a beach.

"Well," said the fish as he swam away, "that certainly lightens my load."

But Avon and Edward could still see nothing.

"Are we in the fish anymore?" asked Avon.

"Not sure," said Edward. "I'm hoping it's nighttime. We'll have to wait and see if daylight comes."

"What if it doesn't?" asked Avon.

"Then perhaps we're still in the fish."

"I just wish," said Avon, "I was brighter."

"Just promise me you'll write about this whole adventure."

"What would its title be?"

"I'd call it *Dialogue: The Dark Side of Writing.*"

"Sounds enlightening," agreed Avon.

CHAPTER SEVENTEEN

In Which Avon, in the End,
Has an Idea

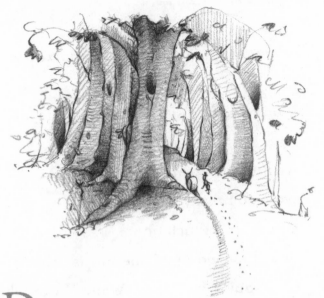

Dawn came.

Edward woke first. "Avon, good news. It's the next day!"

Avon looked around. "It sure looks an awful lot like yesterday to me."

"The point is," said Edward, "I think we'll be able to get home by tomorrow."

"I thought you just said that tomorrow was today."

"Avon, I was just mentioning the next day."

"Whatever happened to today?"

"Avon, you really are in a daze!"

"Exactly. But which one?"

Edward looked up. "The sun is shining."

"I love Sundays," cried Avon. "I can take the day off from my writing!"

The two friends left the beach, entered a forest, and headed for home. It was a long, slow journey, during which time nothing happened—except talking, thinking, feeling, sleeping, waking, and finally, eating. But at last Avon and Edward reached their tree.

"Edward," said Avon, "everything is exactly the way it was when we left."

"Did you think it would change?"

"I suppose I did. I'm very disappointed."

"Why?"

"As a writer, I'd like to bring some change

to the world. But if I can't write, maybe the world can do the changing for itself."

"I suspect it will. It's just a question of paying attention."

"True enough," agreed Avon. "If you don't pay anything, you're not likely to get any change back."

"I just hope," said Edward, "you'll finally be able to write something."

"Actually, since I've already written *Something* and all it did was get us to the sea, I've decided not to write *Something* anymore but to instead write a book about my life. I'm hoping that writing will allow me to find myself."

"I had no idea you were lost," said Edward. "Have you got a title yet?"

"*A Life Lived Backward.*"

"What kind of book will it be?"

"My autobiography."

"Why?"

"I suppose of all writing, it would be most automatic. Or do you think I should write a biography?"

"There's a huge difference," Edward pointed out. "An *auto*biography is about all the things you *ought* to have done. A *bio*graphy is about all the things you should have said *bye* to."

"That makes sense," said Avon.

"Only if you sell the book," warned Edward.

Avon found a new piece of paper and was

about to start writing again when he sighed and said, "I have to admit my thoughts are still in a muddle."

"Avon!" cried Edward. "That's exactly where a writer should be. After all, creatures generally have nothing to do with their beginnings. And it's not often they consider their ends. But in between there's all that

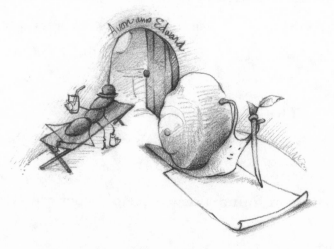

muddle. The writer's job is to write about the muddle."

"Are you saying," said Avon, "that since I'm always in a muddle . . ."

"It proves you are a writer."

"But I have just one more question I've been worried about," said Avon. "Where *do* writers get their ideas?"

"Avon, that's the question most often asked of writers. But you see, writers don't get ideas. They *give* ideas."

"Ah!" cried Avon. "Now I understand!" Then on his paper—with great care—he wrote *Idea*. But he didn't just write it, he added curlicues, extra lines, doodads, doodles, cross-hatching, and all kinds of bits and pieces. Then he gave it to Edward.

Edward gazed at it admiringly. "Avon, I've never seen a writer write such an original idea."

And Avon, muddled as ever, but content at last, beamed.